JULIE

A Magic School for Girls Chapter Book

A.M. Luzzader

Illustrated by Anna Hilton

Published by Knowledge Forest Press
P.O. Box 6331
Logan, UT 84341

Ebook ISBN-13: 978-1-949078-38-1
Paperback ISBN-13: 978-1-949078-37-4

Cover design by Sleepy Fox Studio

Editing by Chadd VanZanten

Interior illustrations by Anna Hilton

CONTENTS

CHAPTER 1
MOONBEAM

Julie Rose lay on her stomach, dangling one of her red hair ribbons over the side of her bed so that her black kitten, Moonbeam, could play with it. Moonbeam had big green eyes, long whiskers, and a little pink nose. The kitten swatted at the ribbon, but then stumbled and fell over the way kittens often do.

Julie laughed at the kitten. "Oh Moonbeam," she said, "You are so cute."

Just then, Julie's mom called from the other room. "Julie, it's time for school."

Julie frowned and flipped her long blond hair over her shoulder. "I guess I have to go, kitten," she told Moonbeam.

Julie was attending Annette McGill's School of Magic for Magically Gifted Girls, which was also known as Miss Annie's Magic School for short. Julie enjoyed learning about magic spells and potions, but on that day, Julie wanted to stay home.

It wasn't that Julie didn't like Miss Annie's Magic School. As a matter of fact, she liked it quite a bit. The teachers were all nice. Her best friends, Bailey and Kate, went to the same school. And Julie wanted to grow up to be a powerful witch, like her mom. Before she had turned eight, Julie had gone to a regular non-magic school. Eight years old was the age when girls could attend Miss Annie's Magic School, and Julie liked magic school much better than ordinary grade school.

Not all girls got to go to a magic school. Not all girls believed in magic, for one thing, and of course if you didn't believe in magic, you wouldn't learn much at a magic school. And not all girls lived near a magic school. And so Julie felt lucky to be a student at Annette McGill's School of Magic for Magically Gifted Girls.

But Julie had also just recently gotten her kitten, Moonbeam, for her eighth birthday. Julie didn't like leaving little Moonbeam at home. It seemed like the kitten was growing up so fast, and Julie didn't want to miss out. When she was supposed to be learning about potions, she wondered if Moonbeam was napping. When her class was learning about the history of magic, Julie was thinking about playing hide-and-seek with Moonbeam.

Cats were very good to have if you wanted to grow up to be a witch. In fact, most grown-up witches owned cats or some other kind of pet. A witch's pet was called a "familiar." Familiars such as cats were said to help witches to cast more powerful magical spells.

Most witches owned black cats, like Moonbeam, but that was only a coincidence. Black was a popular color among witches, and most people love cats. However, witches could have pets of any color to help them cast spells. A green parrot, blue chameleon, yellow snake, or even a tiny orange and white hamster could be a familiar.

Julie stroked the soft, black fur on Moonbeam's back. Then she sighed and sat up. At least Miss Annie's Magic School would teach her how to be a real witch, Julie thought, and then she could spend all day with Moonbeam.

"I'll be back after school," Julie told her kitten, leaving behind the red ribbon for Moonbeam to play with. The little black kitten watched Julie go, then pounced on the ribbon.

CHAPTER 2
A NEW LESSON

Julie always walked to Miss Annie's Magic School with her two best friends, Kate and Bailey. Kate had short black hair. Bailey wore pink glasses and had curly hair. Julie was glad that she and her friends lived close enough to attend Miss Annie's Magic School together. The three friends talked and laughed as they walked to school.

The school building was a large old mansion built from red brick. It was a tall building with many fancy windows, chimneys, and towers. Green leafy vines clung to the walls. On the tallest part of the tallest roof, there stood an iron weather vane with a bat on top. Julie loved the friendly warmth of the building, but sometimes wondered if it might be haunted.

Julie and Bailey both had Miss Betsy Bumble for their teacher that year, but Kate was in Mr. Jack Jasper's class down the hall. Miss Betsy was a kind teacher who was short and round with pretty silver hair that she usually wore in an up-do. Like all the teacher's at Miss Annie's Magic School, Miss Betsy wore a tall witch's hat, which showed that she had graduated from a magic university.

As they climbed the front stairs of the school, the girls saw Miss Annie greeting students at the large front doors. Miss Annie was, of course, the director of Annette McGill's School of Magic for Magically

Gifted Girls. She was a tall, thin, and very dignified witch, with a long face, long nose, and long, flowing hair that was as white as snow. Miss Annie wore a black, close-fitting witch's dress and the tall, wide-brimmed hat of a master witch.

"Good morning, Julie, Kate, and Bailey," said Miss Annie, bowing slightly to the girls.

"Good morning, Miss Annie!" cried the girls.

"Have a magical day," said Miss Annie. It was her favorite greeting.

"Thank you, Miss Annie!" they replied. "We will!"

Julie and her classmates didn't wear witch's hats, because they hadn't graduated yet, though Julie knew she would like to wear one someday. As Julie thought about this, she began wondering what Moonbeam would look like in a hat. She pictured the tiny black cat with a tiny cute witch's hat with a green bow propped on his head. It would be so adorable!

Julie sighed thinking about it.

"Did you say something?" Kate asked as they made their way through the halls of the school.

"No," said Julie. "I was just thinking about Moonbeam."

"Oh," said Kate, but she didn't say anything else.

Bailey and Kate were used to Julie talking about Moonbeam. Julie's friends liked Moonbeam a lot, too, but no one liked or thought of Moonbeam as much as Julie.

So while Julie didn't wear a witch's hat, she wore the school uniform for Annette McGill's School of Magic for Magically Gifted Girls. It was a crisp white shirt, a dark skirt or slacks, a necktie or bow, and special shoes. The uniform not only identified students of Miss Annie's Magic School, but it was also meant to help keep them from accidental spills or magical accidents while they learned about spells and potions.

Julie's friend Kate didn't care for the uniforms. Kate was very artistic, and she preferred wearing bright colors, lots of layers, and sparkling jewelry. Julie liked the uniform because she knew that she would learn to be a witch at Miss Annie's Magic School for Girls, and then she could spend all day with Moonbeam.

"I'm so excited for today," said Bailey. "I can hardly wait for class."

Julie's friend Bailey was always excited for magic school. Bailey was one of the smartest girls in class. At the beginning of the year, some girls had teased Bailey about being a know-it-all and that had made Julie feel sad. She hated seeing her friends feel bad. That was one of the reasons she liked cats so much. Cats never made people feel bad. You wouldn't catch Moonbeam teasing anyone. Sure, Moonbeam might pounce on you or hide from you under the bed, but he would never say something rude! Of course he wouldn't. Cats can't talk!

"What are you so excited about?" asked Kate. "Is

there something different happening or are you just excited for a regular day of school?"

"Julie knows," said Bailey. "Our class is learning something new today. It's going to be awesome."

When Julie heard her own name, she stopped thinking about Moonbeam and started paying attention to Bailey.

"We're learning something new today?" Julie asked.

"Yes," said Bailey. "Don't you remember? Today is our introduction to flying broomsticks!"

When Julie heard this, she wished even more that she had stayed home. In fact, she hoped that Bailey was mistaken. Julie hoped her class was not going to learn about broomsticks or getting on broomsticks or, worst of all, flying on broomsticks. Julie hoped they'd learn more spells, potion recipes, or about crystal balls. To Julie, anything would be better than flying broomsticks!

"Our class is learning about flying broomsticks next week," said Kate. "Do you think it will be fun or scary?"

"Oh, don't worry," said Bailey. "Julie and I will tell you all about it! Right, Julie?"

But Julie didn't say anything, and she had even forgotten all about Moonbeam for the moment.

Kate went down the hall to her class while Julie and Bailey went to their class. When they arrived at their classroom, there were twenty-eight broomsticks stacked against the wall. Enough for each girl in the class.

"This is bad," Julie whispered to herself. "This is very, very bad.

CHAPTER 3
JULIE'S SECRET

Julie didn't like to talk about it much. In fact, she liked to keep it a secret as much as possible, but she didn't know how that would be doable now that the class was learning about flying on broomsticks.

Julie was scared of heights.

Being high up--on mountains, bridges, or skyscrapers--made Julie feel awful. Even being on the top bunk of her cousin's bed made Julie nervous. When Julie was high up, her hands shook and her knees quivered. She felt dizzy and her mouth would dry up. When she was up high, all Julie could think of was falling.

Julie wasn't sure why she was scared of heights. Maybe it was because Julie had fallen out of her crib when she was a toddler and broken her arm. Julie didn't know for sure. All Julie knew was that she liked being on the ground.

On the first day of class at Miss Annie's Magic School, Miss Betsy had made all the desks and chairs dance and fly around in the air, with the students still sitting in them. The other students thought this was a lot of fun, but not Julie. She didn't like it at all. Julie had clung to her desk as if her life depended on it, even though she was only a few feet in the air.

And so when Julie walked into Miss Betsy's class that day and saw the broomsticks, she immediately turned pale, and she felt a lump in her throat.

Bailey noticed right away. "Julie, are you okay?" she asked.

"It's just--those," said Julie, motioning toward the broomsticks.

"I know, isn't it great?" Bailey asked. "We finally get to fly on broomsticks."

Julie was surprised at how Bailey could possibly think that something so scary could be fun. But then again, Julie's kitten, Moonbeam, loved heights, too.

Moonbeam loved to climb. Moonbeam loved to be high up. He climbed up the bookcases, knocking books and knick-knacks to the floor. He jumped up on top of the kitchen cupboards where no one could reach him. He climbed places he wasn't supposed to, like when he climbed up the drapes in the living room. Moonbeam could even leap up and balance on the top edge of Julie's bedroom door!

Moonbeam loved high places, but Julie wondered if Moonbeam might be afraid of flying.

"It's not great," whispered Julie to Bailey as they took their seats. "You know I'm afraid of heights!"

Bailey put a hand to her mouth and gasped. "Oh, Julie! I'm sorry, I forgot! Maybe it won't be so bad. We will probably start by practicing close to the ground."

"Really?" said Julie nervously. "I hope so!"

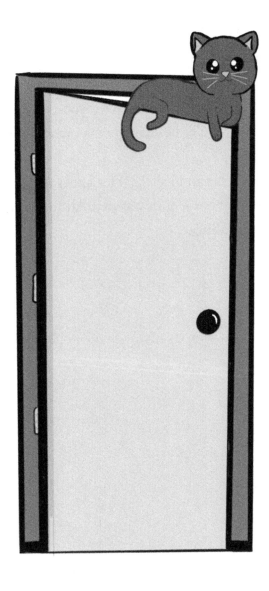

But then Miss Betsy spoke to the class with a twinkle in her eye. "I see you've all noticed the broomsticks. If you pay close attention to what I teach you, by the end of the week you'll all have your very own broomstick and you'll be flying high and zipping through the sky!"

Julie's hands began to shake. Her knees quivered. She felt dizzy and her mouth was dry. All Julie could think about was falling.

CHAPTER 4

THE FIRST LESSON

Miss Betsy led all her students to the school playground. Each student had a broomstick in hand, including Julie.

"Now, class," said Miss Betsy. "We're in for some fun today."

"This isn't what I call fun!" Julie whispered to Bailey.

"Try not to worry," replied Bailey.

But worrying was the only thing Julie could manage to do!

"Before we begin," said Miss Betsy, "I will show you what we'll be learning. You've all seen witches flying on broomsticks before, but maybe you haven't seen exactly what the witches are doing while they're flying. Try to watch closely as I fly my broomstick, and then we'll talk about it more when I'm back on the ground."

"I don't want to look," said Julie, covering her eyes.

Miss Betsy's magic broom had a crooked and twisted handle. It looked like her broomstick was very old and very well used. But it was very nice-looking, too, with long bristles of yellow straw tied together with a dark purple ribbon. It hovered in the air, as if waiting to fly. Miss Betsy threw one leg over the broomstick. Then she sat on the broomstick with one leg on either side. The broomstick seemed to defy gravity as it hovered, despite the added weight of Miss Betsy.

With a sudden woosh, the broomstick took off into the air.

"Wahooo," yelled Miss Betsy.

Miss Betsy and the broomstick zoomed up into the sky, climbing higher and higher. Bailey watched in amazement. All Julie noticed was that Miss Betsy was holding on with only one hand.

"Just watching is going to make me sick," Julie said to Bailey. She felt dizzy and she held onto Bailey's arm so that she wouldn't fall down.

Together they watched their teacher soaring through the air. Miss Betsy wasn't content to just fly here and there, however. She dipped and zipped and flipped and looped. She did all kinds of air acrobatics.

Finally, Miss Betsy and her broomstick floated down to the ground, where it kicked up a small cloud of dust. The broomstick slowed down and came to a stop at last. Then Miss Betsy gently hopped off.

Her cheeks were pink and her eyes were glistening. "Isn't flying grand?" she asked, catching her breath. "Oh, I can't wait for you girls to soar up among the clouds. Now gather close."

The students circled around Miss Betsy. Julie felt very nervous.

"Flying on a broomstick is similar to riding a bike," said Miss Betsy. "You have to balance on the broomstick, for example, like when you ride a bike."

The students nodded.

"But there are some differences, of course," added Miss Betsy. "There are no handlebars to steer, for example. Instead, to turn left or right, you lean to the left or to the right."

"Oh, we have to lean off the broomstick?" said Julie to herself, placing a hand on her clammy forehead.

"To fly lower, you lean forward," explained Miss Betsy. "Does anyone want to guess what to do if you want to fly higher?"

Julie shyly raised her hand.

"Yes, dear?" said Miss Betsy, pointing to Julie. "What do you think?"

"Lean backward?" said Julie quietly.

"That's right!" said Miss Betsy.

Julie thought she might faint. "Why would anyone want to go higher?" she thought.

"Now," said Miss Betsy, "who can tell me how to make a broomstick go faster?"

Bailey raised her hand.

"Yes, Bailey," said Miss Betsy.

"Push downward on the handle," said Bailey.

"That's right, dear," said Miss Betsy with a nod. "Push down on your broomstick handle. And to slow down or stop, you pull up. It's very simple, but don't worry if it seems strange at first. Don't try to resist or fight with your broomstick. You and your broomstick are a team. Your magic and the broomstick work together."

While Julie hadn't always been excited about all the lessons she had learned at Miss Annie's Magic School, this was the first lesson that she didn't want to learn at all.

Julie raised her hand.

"Yes, Julie?" said Miss Betsy.

"I was just wondering," said Julie, "do all witches have to learn to fly on a broomstick?"

Miss Betsy tipped her head. "A witch that doesn't fly on a broomstick? Hmm. You know, I don't think I've ever heard of a witch who didn't. Why do you ask?"

Julie thought about graduating from witch university to become a grown-up witch. Then she'd be able to spend all her time with Moonbeam. She thought there weren't many jobs that allowed you to be with a cat all day. Maybe a pet shop owner or a veterinarian. But Julie really did want to be a witch.

So, she said, "No reason. I was just wondering if this lesson is absolutely mandatory."

"Oh, are you feeling a bit nervous?" Miss Betsy asked. "Don't worry! That's normal. And that is precisely why we begin practicing with our feet on the ground and then fly a couple feet in the air. Don't worry, you'll get the hang of it."

This didn't make Julie feel very much better. Practicing on the ground might be fun. Flying two feet in the air might be okay. But then she would have to fly higher, and that would be awful. What would she do then? Would Julie be the first witch in history who couldn't fly a broomstick?

CHAPTER 5
NOT A SICK DAY

On Monday and Tuesday, the broomstick lessons consisted of the class running around on the playground with their brooms, practicing pushing left and right and forward and back to control the brooms. Even though they stayed on the ground, all the students could sense the magical energy present in the broomsticks. Julie felt okay about this.

"See? I told you," said Bailey as she raced past Julie. "It's fun, huh?"

"I guess so," said Julie. She had to admit it was a little fun.

But toward the end of the second day, Julie started to notice that her broomstick was acting, well, kind of funny.

It kept lifting up a little higher, as though it wanted to take off and climb high into the sky.

Julie asked Miss Betsy about it.

"Hmm, you're very lucky!" said Miss Betsy. "You've got an eager broomstick."

Julie didn't like the sound of that. She would prefer to have a lazy broomstick.

"Some broomsticks just love to fly," Miss Betsy explained.

"Oh no," moaned Julie.

"No, that's a good thing, dear," said Miss Betsy. "It means it will be easy to fly once you're in the sky. These broomsticks all have their own personalities. The bashful ones are the most difficult to fly."

Julie looked down at her broomstick, who even at that moment, was pulling upwards. She would be perfectly comfortable with a bashful broom. Then the two of them could stay close to the ground, where it was nice and safe.

"You're all doing very well," said Miss Betsy. "Tomorrow we'll move on to using the step stools."

Julie groaned. Bailey overheard this and steered her broomstick over to Julie.

"It's just the step stools," said Bailey, patting Julie gently on the shoulder. "We won't be very high."

"It's high enough," said Julie. "Besides, I know what comes after that. First, it's the step stool and then it's the whole sky. I want nothing to do with it."

"You're just feeling nervous," said Bailey. "That's okay. Everyone feels nervous about some things some of the time. I think you'll feel better after you try it though."

"I don't want to try it," said Julie. "Never, ever, never!"

The next morning before school, Julie gathered up her things, but when she grabbed her broom, her hands began to shake. And so Julie decided to try and see if she could take a sick day. But her mom always made her drink that icky dragon nail powder juice when she was sick. That was one of the tastes that Julie hated. Her friend, Kate, had lots of tastes that she hated, but Julie only had a few. Still, it was worth drinking dragon nail powder juice, if it meant she didn't have to fly in the sky.

But when she told her mom that she wasn't feeling well, her mom came over and looked into Julie's eyes. She looked at Julie's tongue. She put her wrist on Julie's neck. Then Julie's mom wiggled her nose and waved her hand over Julie's head. A few little sparks of magic floated here and there.

"No," said Julie's mom, "you definitely aren't sick."

That was the problem with having a mom who was also a witch and could do magic. They knew all kinds of magic for things, such as telling if a kid is really sick or if they are faking it.

"Well, I feel sick," said Julie.

"Is something wrong?" asked Julie's mom.

Julie looked at her broomstick again. "Well, it's just--," and she nodded at her magic broomstick.

"You're scared to fly, aren't you?" her mom asked.

"It's my fear of heights," said Julie. "I'm so scared I'll fall."

"Miss Betsy won't let any of you fly without a magic spell to protect you from falling," said Julie's mom. "Even if you did fall off your broom, you would just float gently back to the ground. You won't be hurt."

"That's what my ears hear, but that's not what my brain tells me. I'm too scared to do it. Please don't make me," said Julie.

"I know you're scared," said her mom, "but broomstick flying is an essential skill for becoming a witch. You still want to be a witch, don't you?"

Julie thought about it. In addition to getting to have a familiar cat with you all day long, there were a lot of other really cool things about being a witch. Witches used magic to help people. Master witches could see into the future and visit the past. And, of course, Halloween for witches was way better than Christmas.

And so, even though she didn't always like magic school, she did really want to be a witch.

"Yes, I still want to be a witch," said Julie.

"Can you just give it a try then?" her mom asked. "I know you're scared, but can you still try?"

"Okay," Julie said glumly. She wished she didn't have to do it, but if it was part of being a witch she'd at least try.

CHAPTER 6
STEP STOOLS

Julie didn't know where Miss Betsy had gotten them, but when the class went out to the playground with their broomsticks, there were twenty-eight step stools scattered around the grounds.

Julie and Bailey picked stools close to each other.

"All right, class," said Miss Betsy. "Today, we're going to take to the air, though we won't be flying very high. Just a couple feet off the ground. We'll use the step stools to help us get going. Go ahead and practice the skills you've been learning."

Julie noticed nervously that her broomstick was hovering a little higher in the air that day. She watched as Bailey climbed up the step stool, positioned her broom, and then stepped off the stool. Her broom floated about two feet in the air.

"Oh wow, this is amazing," said Bailey. She leaned forward and Bailey and her broom zipped across the playground. Julie watched as she went to the end of the soccer field then turned around and came back.

"Come on, Julie," said Bailey. "Try it. Look, I can

still touch the ground if I need to." Bailey reached a leg down from her broom to show Julie how close the ground still was. All around them the other students had stepped off their step stools and were flying all around. They laughed and hooted, even though they stayed close to the ground.

Bailey came over to help Julie. The step stool had only three steps. Julie took the first step.

"Just two more steps," Bailey said.

Julie blushed. She knew it really wasn't that high, but she was scared anyway. She didn't want to feel scared, but she did! Julie was glad that she had a friend who was kind and patient.

Julie took the second step. Her hands began to shake.

"Just one more," said Bailey. "You can do it!"

Julie stood on the top step.

"Now just get on your broom," said Bailey.

Julie got on her broom. There was sweat on her forehead and her heart pounded. Julie looked down at the ground. She knew it was only a few feet, but when she looked down the distance seemed to multiply by one hundred.

The broom was tugging forward in her hands. She knew her broomstick wanted to fly.

"Step off the stool," said Bailey. "Go fly!"

Julie looked down again.

"No, no, no," Julie said and she rushed back down the steps.

Bailey rushed over and gave Julie a hug. "It's okay, Julie," she said. "I'm sorry it's so scary for you."

Julie was embarrassed that everyone else in the class was flying but she couldn't.

Just then, Miss Betsy flew over on her broom.

"Is everything okay, girls?" she asked.

"Yes, yes," said Julie. "I, um, just feel like I need some more practicing on the ground." She began running with her broom.

"I think you've practiced on the ground enough," said Miss Betsy. "It's time to try it off the ground."

"Nope, not quite enough," said Julie urgently. "I need just a bit more." She laughed nervously. "Maybe I have one of those bashful brooms after all." Julie's broom gave a big tug after she said that, but Julie pretended not to notice.

When class ended that day, Julie still had not flown with her broom off of the ground. So she was super worried when Miss Betsy said that the next day they'd be flying in the sky with no limits.

"But of course, since you are beginners, I'll have

some magical spells that will protect you if you fall," said Miss Betsy, "So there's nothing to worry about."

But Julie was worried. Really, really worried. She was trying to think about how she might be able to get out of school the next day, and maybe the next week, too. Would it take a month? How long was the broomstick flying course anyway?

But just then, Miss Betsy passed around a handout that changed everything.

CHAPTER 7
MOONBEAM GOES TO SCHOOL

Julie's mom read the handout that Miss Betsy had given all the students explaining the details of Bring Your Magic Pet to School Day.

"Oh, this is a fun day!" said her mom.

"So, can I really bring Moonbeam to school with me?" asked Julie.

"Yes, of course," her mom answered. "It's one of the best days at Miss Annie's Magic School!"

"And he can stay with me the whole day?" asked Julie.

"Yes," said her mom. "Just be careful and make sure he doesn't get into any trouble."

"Yipee!" cried Julie. "A whole day at school with Moonbeam!"

Bring Your Magic Pet to School Day almost made Julie forget about the flying broomstick lessons. It was great news. Julie was brushing Moonbeam's black fur coat and picking out a pretty bow to put on his collar while she talked to her mom.

"Okay," said her mom, "after you show Moonbeam to your classmates, you should keep him in his kitty carrier. Moonbeam is still just a kitten, which means he is too young to protect himself. Who knows what other kinds of pets will be there. And you know how he loves to climb everything."

"Don't worry," said Julie. "I'll be super careful! I would never let anything happen to Moonbeam. Isn't that right, kitty?" Julie nuzzled the kitten, as he playfully swatted at her nose.

Julie knew that the next day of school would be the best ever, and for the first time in a long time, she couldn't wait to go to school.

When Julie met Bailey and Kate to go to school the next day, she had Moonbeam in a cat carrier. Bailey had her pet dog Woofer on a leash and Kate was carrying a fish bowl in which there was a beta fish named Hop.

"Is that Moonbeam in the kitty carrier?" asked Bailey.

"Yes," answered Julie. She was thrilled. "Isn't this great? I wish I could bring Moonbeam to school every day."

"Me, too!" said Kate and Bailey.

When Julie and Bailey got to their classroom, they saw pets of all sorts. Miss Betsy had set aside the morning for the students to take turns introducing their pets. The students were also able to ask each other questions about their pets.

Pamela had a parakeet in a little travel cage made of wire.

"Parakeets are very fine pets for witches!" said Miss Betsy. "They can often sense danger before we can."

Liz had a giant toad in a plastic habitat.

Miss Betsy reached in and patted the toad on its big, bumpy head. "Toads may not look very intelligent, but they are very wise and give very good advice to witches."

When Bailey showed Woofer to the class, Miss Betsy said, "Dogs make very good familiars for witches because they have an excellent sense of smell and very good hearing."

When it was her turn, Julie pulled Moonbeam from his carrier and held him up for the class to see.

The students said "ooo!" and "ahh!" Moonbeam looked around the class with wide, curious eyes.

"This is Moonbeam," said Julie proudly. "His favorite things are chasing toys, taking naps, and cat treats, but he likes climbing most of all."

Miss Betsy said, "Does anyone have any questions about Moonbeam?"

"How did you come up with his name?" asked Heather.

"On the first night I got Moonbeam," answered Julie, "we were playing on my bed, and the moon was shining through my window. Moonbeam opened his big green eyes and stared at the moon for the longest time. So, I named him Moonbeam."

"How old is Moonbeam?" Rebecca asked.

"Six months," said Julie.

Then Miss Betsy talked to the class. "Most of you already know that cats are a popular familiar for witches because they are naturally magical. Julie, thank you very much for sharing your pet with us today. Make sure you keep him in his carrier. I wouldn't want such a sweet little kitten to get loose and get lost in the school, or get chased around by one of the other pets."

"I will," said Julie, but this was easier to say than it was to do.

CHAPTER 8
A LITTLE PROBLEM

The students got to keep their pets with them for the entire day if they wanted. Julie's mom had offered to pick up Moonbeam after the presentation, but Julie wanted Moonbeam to stay all day. And she wished Moonbeam could come out of his kitty carrier, too. She knew if she took Moonbeam out of the carrier, he might get away or cause trouble, but Julie still wished he could come out. Instead, she poked her fingers through the openings to pet Moonbeam and to give him treats.

Even though it had been a special day for the students, they still had to do their regular lessons. So, in the afternoon, Miss Betsy took everyone outside for more broomstick flying practice.

Julie had so much fun during Bring Your Magic Pet to School Day, she had completely forgotten about the flying broomstick lessons. But as she carried Moonbeam in his carrier outside, she began to feel her fear building.

"I don't want to do this," she told Bailey.

While the other students were practicing zooming through the air, Julie sat on the ground with her broomstick. Miss Betsy encouraged her to participate, but Julie was simply too afraid. She really wanted to learn how to be a good witch, and it made her sad that she couldn't get over her fear of heights.

When class was over, Julie and Bailey made their way out of the school with their broomsticks. Bailey had Woofer on his leash and Julie had Moonbeam in his kitty carrier. Kate had a dentist appointment that afternoon, so her mom had already picked Kate and Hop up from the school. As Bailey and Julie walked through the halls, Woofer got very excited because he knew they were going outside. He leaped and barked and wrapped the leash around Bailey's legs. Bailey struggled to keep him under control. She felt bad that Julie was sad about the flying broomstick lessons. Even though Bailey was distracted by Woofer, she tried to make Julie feel better.

"I was thinking," said Bailey. "The thing you're most afraid of is falling, right?"

Thinking about falling made a lump form in Julie's throat, so she couldn't speak. She nodded.

"But Miss Betsy says it's perfectly safe because she has cast a safety spell on our broomsticks to keep us from falling and getting hurt," said Bailey.

"Yes, that's true," said Julie. "And while I trust Miss Betsy, something in my brain just doesn't believe it. I can't help it. It's too scary."

"Right," said Bailey as Woofer jumped and pulled at the leash. "What I was thinking was, what if you saw someone else fall and land safely? Then maybe you wouldn't be so scared of falling."

"Maybe," said Julie. "But who is going to risk falling?"

"I'll do it," said Bailey. "I've read all about the safety spell, and I have no doubt it will work. I'll just fly up and then fall off on purpose. Then you'll be able to see that it is okay to fall."

"Really? You'd do that for me?" Julie asked.

"Of course!" said Bailey. "You, me, and Kate all need to grow up and be witches together and how can we do that if you can't fly on a broomstick? I've got your back, Julie."

Julie couldn't believe how thoughtful Bailey was being, but she still felt nervous. But if she could see that the safety spell really did work, maybe her mind would stop making her feel so scared.

"You're sure the spell will work?" Julie asked. "You won't get hurt?"

"Miss Betsy's spells are super strong," said Bailey. "There's nothing to worry about. Let's go to the playground before we go home."

"Okay, then," said Julie. "But be careful and don't go up too high."

"Deal," said Bailey. "Um, but can you hold Woofer while I fly?"

"Sure," said Julie.

Since school was out for the day, there weren't very many people at the playground. Bailey handed Woofer's leash to her. Julie held onto Moonbeam's carrier in one hand, Woofer's leash in the other, and she had her broomstick under one arm.

Bailey got on her broom and slowly began flying into the air.

Woofer jumped and barked as he watched Bailey climbing higher into the sky.

"Don't go too high," Julie yelled, holding tight to Woofer's leash.

Bailey stopped flying. "Okay," she said, "here I come!"

She tilted off her broom and slid off, but she didn't fall! Instead, the broomstick stayed in the air, while Bailey floated slowly back to the ground. The safety spell worked!

Seeing Bailey in the sky like that made Woofer pull even harder on the leash. He lunged forward and it jerked Julie forward. This made her drop Moonbeam's carrier. The carrier hit the ground and the lid burst open.

In a panic, Moonbeam darted out. Then the kitten saw Woofer, leaping around and barking. Moonbeam puffed up until he was at least three times his normal size. His tail, usually thin and graceful, looked like a big black hairbrush! Moonbeam hissed and dashed away.

"Moonbeam, come back!" Julie yelled.

But the kitten had already found his way to a nearby tree and was climbing up, up, up.

CHAPTER 9
THE RESCUE

After Bailey landed gently on the ground, she rushed over to take Woofer's leash back from Julie.

"Oh, no," said Bailey, "Moonbeam got away."

The two girls ran to the base of the tree that Moonbeam had climbed. The kitten was so high up. They almost couldn't see him. They could only see his tiny face and green eyes peeking out from behind a branch high up. In his panic, he had raced to nearly the top of the tree, and now that he was there, Moonbeam looked back at the ground and realized he couldn't get down. The kitten mewed sadly and desperately.

"Moonbeam!" Julie yelled.

"I'll fly up and get him for you," said Bailey. But

then she realized that her broom was stuck up in the sky where she'd jumped off it. This must have been part of Miss Betsy's safety spell.

Julie knew what she had to do. She said nothing, but she picked up her broomstick, and without thinking, she got on it and took off.

"Julie!" cried Bailey. "Be careful!"

Julie hadn't been practicing her broomstick controls as much as the other students. At first, she veered too far to the left.

Bailey cupped her hands at her mouth and shouted, "Lean to your right!"

Julie leaned to the right, but she steered too far and had to lean to the left again.

"Don't lean so far!" Bailey yelled. "Slow down!"

Julie knew that she had to push down on the broomstick to slow down, but she got confused and leaned back and accidentally did a loop in the air! Next, she flew way over the tree, then way under it, then all around it. Bailey did her best to help from the ground. Moonbeam meowed and meowed, clinging to the branch with his sharp little claws.

At last Julie steered her broomstick to the branch. It hovered while Julie reassured Moonbeam.

"It's okay, Moonbeam," said Julie. "I'm here. Let me help you." Julie didn't realize it, but she wasn't nervous. Her hands weren't shaking. Her knees weren't quivering. She was very high up in the air, but for some reason, she wasn't scared!

Julie gave Moonbeam a few reassuring pets and then gently plucked him from the branch. Moonbeam was still puffed up and his eyes were wide with fear. Julie set him in her lap and steered the magic broomstick downward. When she returned to the ground, she hopped off and returned Moonbeam to the safety of his carrier. Bailey had scolded Woofer and he was now on his best behavior.

"Julie!" cried Bailey. "You did it! You flew!"

"Oh, wow!" said Julie. "I did. I didn't even think about being scared, I just knew I needed to save Moonbeam."

Miss Betsy had been watching her from the window in her classroom. She ran downstairs and onto the playground. "Jumping jackfrogs!" she cried. "Julie! I'm very proud of you!"

Julie smiled. When she hadn't been thinking about falling, it had been easy to fly. Saving Moonbeam was more important than her fears.

"It wasn't that bad," said Julie, blinking her eyes. "In fact, I might be willing to give it another try."

"Then, let's go," said Bailey.

Miss Betsy ordered Bailey's broom to come back down from the sky. Then she held onto Woofer's leash and watched over Moonbeam's kitty carrier while the two friends practiced flying over the playground on their broomsticks. Julie would always be a little nervous about being up high. However, once she got on her broom, she just took a deep breath and tried not to look down. She reminded herself that if she did fall off her broom that she would float gently to the ground, just like Bailey had.

After a few minutes, Julie started enjoying herself. She began doing dives and turns and all kinds of tricks on her broomstick.

"You're a natural," called Miss Betsy down on the ground.

Julie could sense the broomstick wanting to go faster and higher, and so she let it. She laughed and smiled as she and her broomstick flew all through the sky.

Julie didn't think anything could be more fun than bringing Moonbeam to school, but that was before she learned she could fly! She absolutely loved it. It really was her best day at school ever!

CHAPTER 10
SOME NEW FUN

Kate's class finished the course on broomstick flying the next week. Both Kate's teacher and Miss Betsy instructed the students to practice often, and for once, this was homework that Julie didn't mind doing at all.

One afternoon after school, Julie, Bailey, and Kate, all went for a fly together. They took their brooms through cities and towns, over hills, through the cotton candy clouds, and finally settled into the sky to watch the sun set. Julie was still a little nervous, but she had fun, too.

It was good to know she could graduate from witch university and be a real witch. Maybe she could even become a master witch, like Miss Annie.

As the evening sky turned to pink and purple, the three friends hovered over the city and waited for sunset. Just then, Moonbeam poked his head out of the top of Julie's jacket. The little black kitten purred as he and Julie watched the setting sun. When Moonbeam was a bit bigger, Julie planned to teach him how to sit on the broomstick by himself. And then, when Julie was older, they'd be all set. A witch and her magical cat who could fly wherever they wanted on their magical broomstick.

Kate looked over and noticed Moonbeam. "Bailey!" she said. "Look at Julie and Moonbeam!"

Bailey and Kate giggled at Moonbeam, his little head sticking up through Julie's jacket and his green eyes glowing in the sunlight.

"That's adorable!" said Bailey. "You had him with you this whole time?"

Julie nodded and patted the kitten's head. "Yep. Moonbeam just loves being high up!"

PLEASE LEAVE A REVIEW

Thank you for reading this book. We hope you enjoyed it! We would really appreciate it if you would please take a moment to review *Julie: A Magic School for Girls Chapter Book* on Amazon or other retail sites. Thank you!

WWW.AMLUZZADER.COM

- blog
- freebies
- newsletter
- contact info

OTHER BOOKS BY
A.M. Luzzader

A Magic School for Girls
Chapter Book

For ages
6-8

OTHER BOOKS BY
A.M. Luzzader

 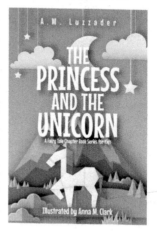

A Fairy Tale Chapter Book Series for Kids

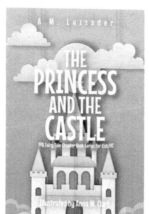

For ages
6-8

OTHER BOOKS BY
A.M. Luzzader

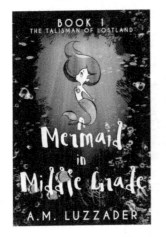 

A Mermaid in Middle Grade
Books 1-3

For ages
8-12

OTHER BOOKS BY
A.M. Luzzader

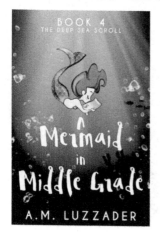 

A Mermaid in Middle Grade
Books 4–6

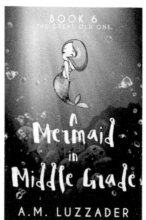

For ages
8-12

ABOUT THE AUTHOR

A.M. Luzzader is an award-winning children's author who writes chapter books and middle grade books. She specializes in writing books for preteens. A.M.'s fantasy adventure series 'A Mermaid in Middle Grade' is a magical coming of age book series for ages 8-12. She is also the author of the 'Hannah Saves the

World' series, which is a children's mystery adventure, also for ages 8-12.

A.M. decided she wanted to write fun stories for kids when she was still a kid herself. By the time she was in fourth grade, she was already writing short stories. In fifth grade, she bought a typewriter at a garage sale to put her words into print, and in sixth grade she added illustrations. Now that she has decided what she wants to be when she grows up, A.M. writes books for girls and boys full time. She was selected as the Writer of the Year in 2019-2020 by the League of Utah Writers.

A.M. is the mother of a 10-year-old and a 13-year-old who often inspire her stories. She lives with her husband and children in northern Utah. She is a devout cat person and avid reader.

A.M. Luzzader's books are appropriate for ages 5-12. Her chapter books are intended for kindergarten to third grade, and her middle grade books are for third grade through sixth grade. Find out more about A.M., sign up to receive her newsletter, and get special offers at her website: www.amluzzader.com.

facebook.com/a.m.luzzader
amazon.com/author/amluzzader

ABOUT THE ILLUSTRATOR

Anna Hilton is sixteen years old and has lived in Utah all of her life. She enjoys art, dancing, and spending time with her friends. Anna loves to read novels and to draw pictures of everything she sees.

Made in the USA
Middletown, DE
20 October 2021